WAKING

By the same author

EQUINOX
WINTER JOURNEY
KONEK LANDING
B
DAYS
NELLY'S VERSION

Non-fiction
PATRIARCHAL ATTITUDES
TRAGEDY AND SOCIAL EVOLUTION
LITTLE EDEN

WAKING

Eva Figes

Pantheon Books
New York

LIBRARY OF CONGRESS CATALOGING IN PUBLICATION DATA

Figes, Eva.
Waking.

I. Title.
PR6056.I46w3   1981   823'.914   81-14078
ISBN 0-394-52325-3   AACR2

Manufactured in the United States of America
First American Edition

1

Light. Glowing yellow. It spills into the room of wavering shadows and forms a pool on the floor. The pool of melted butter oozes across the floorboards as a soft gust of air slowly lifts the cloth hung over the window; luminous now, it bulges inward with the motion of a half-filled sail filled by a gentle breeze running across the surface of the water on a stifling afternoon. The window was open all night. It must have been hot. I am warm now, and sticky.

The pool of light on the floor expands, flows outward to touch the leg of a chair and then suddenly fades, as though liquid had soaked into the wood and dried. The curtain hangs limp and dull. But now it moves inward once more, billowing with the wind heard in the tree outside, wonderfully luminous. And a spot of light is now dancing on the ceiling, trembling with an intensity of light,

5

perhaps a mysterious form of living, capable of changing shape, of hovering without wings or limbs, without taking in food. I watch it for a long time as it shines, quavering, without leaving the dark corner of the ceiling.

The curtains have changed, do not look as I remember them from yesterday. The cloth has no colour, nor do the leaves and flowers, which are black curved shapes standing out from a luminous ground as the light comes through. I am puzzled by this. I remember that last night I saw a curtain which had red and blue flowers picked out from trailing green leaves. I watch how the black shapes of leaves and flowers flow in the wind-blown luminosity and count the colours in my memory. I am determined not to be tricked. Some time in the future the disparity will be justified.

Before I opened my eyes I heard a cock crow. The shrill sound tore through the dark remnants of sleep, hustled the last shadow of a dream from my head and brought me back into this room, with sunlight spilling in. Now I lie in the silence, listening to small sounds, the hum of an insect, air breathing with a heavy sigh through branches which shadow the house, leaves falling in shadow on wall and sunlit floor as the wind stirs the fringes. Inside the house I listen intently to the creak of a floorboard, a dull almost inaudible thud, the sound of mattress and bed-spring as somebody turns in sleep, murmuring an inaudible word. I want to get up. I listen for sounds through the wall, for the inaudible murmur to become sharp and clear, shaped by consonants, extended to a whole sentence which, perhaps ending in the lift of a question mark would by its very intonation tell me, even before I heard the sound of her voice, several rungs higher than his, that both were awake. But no: the small sounds subside into silence. I must lie here, waiting. I am not allowed to get up and begin the day by disturbing them.

Time passes very slowly. I begin to count seconds, to experience the length of a minute. I have been taught how to do it. I must not gabble, counting the numbers as fast as I know how: each number must be paced out in a steady rhythm, like a pulse. I reach the end of a minute, out of breath, my mouth dry. Nothing has changed. The whorl of light still hovers on the ceiling, dancing on the same spot as though invisibly spellbound. Air moves through the shadow of leaves and lifts the thin cotton drawn across the open window.

Time is larger than me. The whole day which now stretches ahead is an inconceivable mass, heavy as clouds.

Now I can hear birdsong. Outside in the garden where I want to be birds are singing in the trees, high up in the leaves above my head. I want to get up. I want to run out of doors and begin the day by running through the long wet grass with nothing on my feet but sandals and my arms and legs bare, I am ready to begin yet another long summer day by wading through long wet grass still steeped in cool blue shadow, with the sun only a distant sparkle glimpsed through the dark moving foliage of the high tree and cobwebs in the corner by the old woodshed glistening with a thousand small beads of water, round, holding the light, each globe holding the world in bending light, as I move, running under the trees as drops of water run down my bare skin to trickle into the space between bare foot and the leather sole of my shoe, as it gleams on

7

the leathery leaves of the roses and falls in a sudden shower from the lilac bush by the gate. I want, I want, I cannot wait. Even now birds are pecking at the berries, how they sing while I lie here in a triumphant chorus from the topmost branches of the cherry tree. Who knows what rich round pickings lie hidden close to earth under the leaves of the strawberry bed? And while I lie here the birds are at work with their beaks, black slugs lie hidden under the leaves and the sun is rising, rising. Soon the grass will be dry and the pools of blue shadows full of the remnants of night, of silence, whispering unspoken secrets will have dried when the sun is high in the blue sky and the everyday dust rises in the bright glare of voices. I want to get up, now, now, while the whole day waits ahead like a huge ship, an ocean-going liner, and the secret garden waits, still cool in its pool of deep bluish shadows, and damp with its glistening beads of water which nobody has disturbed. It hangs on the cobwebs by the woodshed, soaks into the hidden earth from each bending grass helm, runs into the pollen-dusty calyx of the rose.

But I lie, counting seconds. One, two, three, four. Clock time goes slowly, a minute could be an hour. Indoor time goes slowly, so that within the house nobody stirs, I hear no sound; meanwhile the time of the wind in the trees stirs like quicksilver, running through the leaves in the trees whose shadows move on my floor, throbbing wildly in the feathers and beaks of birds, running to ground in trembling drops of water which had hung, tremulous, on the lip of a rose.

I lie. Listen. The glowing pool of light runs across the

floorboards. Inside the house nobody stirs. I want to get up, but I am not allowed to do so. Not yet. Not till I hear voices through the wall, more than a murmur followed by silence. His deep voice speaking words in sequence, the other voice several shades higher breaking with laughter. I listen for the creatures to stir from their underwater slumber. I do not know them. I have been in their room on other mornings, when the sound of the sea far below came through the open window and the room lay washed in shadow which subdued the rumpled white sheets in which both lay, their shapes alien, large, short black hairs growing from olive skin, soft bulges of flesh from which an unexpected smell of must was very strong, heavy eyelids and the flesh of cheeks crumpled like blankets. I do not know those creatures. They are warm, loving, they fold me into their arms, into the folds of the bedclothes from which the smell comes, so I do not like to say to the woman, I do not know you, though her eyes are odd and she has too much hair, it runs from her head all over the pillow and when she lies with her head on her arm watching me with those odd, heavy-lidded eyes a dark bushy tuft becomes visible in her armpit while she smiles oddly, not so much at me whom she is watching but into the dark underwater dream which still lurks in her black pupils like a drug, while her heavy eyelids droop. And the other is wild, a satyr, his laughter lifted to the heavy rafters of the low ceiling, the bedsprings bounce with his wild spirits, he will toss me upward till I shriek with excitement, begging him to stop, I am not sure which I want, only that I cannot cope with such intense pleasure, it runs through me like electricity, my

9

limbs tingle, my stomach is left behind as I see, far, far below his white teeth exposed under the thick dark moustache which tickles, her sleep-sodden face sunk in the pillow on which is strewn hair like a tangle of sea-weed left behind by the tide, as I fly, laughter forced out of me, shrieking, sure that my head will hit the dark rafters even as I begin to fall.

No. I do not know those creatures beyond the wall, while I lie listening for the first sounds to come from their room. A floorboard creaks. Outside, the wind sighs in the leaves which move in shadow on the floor. The curtain flaps suddenly, hard, like canvas as the bow turns into the wind. From this side of the house I cannot hear the sea, only the green tide surging.

Time passes very slowly. I am warm. The curtain lifts. This time the entire chair is bathed in pale light before it falls back and hangs slack. Now I see a tinge of dark green in the black pattern of the curtains. The colours are coming back. I remember that I heard a cock crow before I opened my eyes. I wish it would crow again, but though I listen, I hear nothing. Only birds singing high up in the cherry tree. By now they will have picked all the best cherries, those turned juicy and black in yesterday's sun. Their song is jubilant. Thinking, it seems to me that the cry I heard of the cock was a cry of triumph. Why? I do not know. Once my father hung silver strips in the branches of the cherry tree to scare off the birds. The tree looked festive, not frightening. How long ago was that? I do not know. How long until I am a year older? I cannot tell. Many hours and days.

I touch the top of my head and, with my legs stiff, knees

touching, push my toes down hard. I am growing. With my arms above my head I can scratch the headboard with my fingertips while my toes touch the bottom of the bed. It is only lately that I have been able to do this. My mother has sewn a band of white ribbon round the bottom hem of my favourite cotton frock, the one I wear here almost every day. It reminds me of the sky at night, because it is blue with small white stars scattered all over. Soon, she says, you will not be able to wear it anymore, because it is getting too short. I was angry, no, I said, no, and stamped my sandalled foot on the dusty path when she said, I shall give the dress away to somebody with a small child. She shrugged. All right, she smiled, and stitched the broad ribbon round the bottom. Her smile told me an uncomfortable and bitter truth I already knew, that it would not be for long, that even with the ribbon round the hem I was still growing. Soon she would give the dress away.

Now I hear something. A large fly is bouncing off the ceiling in an effort to escape. The small black body buzzes with rage, sizzling with impotent fury as it throws itself against the solid mass, only to be thrown back. I think it is a housefly. Now it begins to circle round the room. I am puzzled that its wings are still functioning.

I pull the bedclothes over my head. This is my house, dark, secret and warm. It smells of my body. The smells of my own body comfort me, I find it pleasurable to break wind and then sniff. I do it a second time. I try to plan a house under the bedclothes, from the sloping attic down by my feet to the door where the sheet lets in light by my head. I lift the sheet, look out, and pull it down so that I am lying in almost total darkness. Crouching on my knees, the roofbeam rises with my back, it is spacious, this grey room, from which everybody is excluded, unless I decide to open the door by lifting the edge of the sheet to allow in air, a slit of light. This is my house, I can change its shape at will, arching my spine I see huge unused spaces stretching far below and into the remote darkness beyond my feet. I could move further down if I wished, explore those corners, but this is far enough. I can hear the words in my head now, quite clearly. I who am talking now, but not in a whisper, no need to whisper, I talk calmly to my smooth knee, I lick the place where the scab has peeled off leaving a small white mark, I sniff the skin of my arm, how brown it smells, delicious, it smells of sunlight and yesterday's baking hot afternoon.

My back begins to ache. Hot, my face burns. I lift the edge of the sheet above my head and peer out.

My face is flushed, hair tangles in my eyes. I am breathing fast. Dark spots like little fishes swim in front of my eyes. I blink, they sink to the bottom of the pool and re-emerge. I shut my eyes and watch the inside of my lids, which glow scarlet. A glowing crimson world. I squeeze my lids, relax, and the pattern comes, purple and gold. Squeeze again, ordinary dark red. Squeeze once more and this time it comes, glaring zigzags of acid green, silver light and black. I bounce on the mattress in triumph, then stop, panting for breath. I have a theatre behind my eyelids, and the show I like best is a glaring pattern of bright white and acid green. I can always make it come.

Now I hear footsteps, voices murmuring low through the wall. Soon I will get up. I will wear my blue frock with the tiny white stars. My arms and legs will be bare. I will walk through the long grass and perhaps it will still be wet. Water will run into my instep. Perhaps this afternoon the old man with the scythe will come and cut the long grass between the fruit trees. He talks to me as he works, rubbing the curved blade to make it sharp before he swings. He tells me to keep out of the way and I jump, laughing, as though he was going to cut me down. I shriek with laughter, pretending to be afraid, as though I was going to topple with the blades of grass, they lie on their sides like toy soldiers, green swathes gleam silver, among them lie the heads of daisies and fat yellow dandelions bleeding white juice from their cut stalks. The old man talks to me as he works, whistling through his teeth as the blade goes swish, swish, but he never laughs. Nor does he smile. The flat swathes of grass gleam in the sun, and he watches me oddly from the corner of his eye as his thin body swings the curved scythe which seems too large for him, and his old clothes hang on him, bleached with age to the colour of bone.

I will run. I will make a daisy chain. I will find a snail and see how it moves slowly forward, leaving a thin trail of shining slime. I will crawl under the bushes into my secret house. I will blow a dandelion clock and watch how the spores fly up, up into the air. I will collect small stones from the footpath and put them into my jewel box because I know them to be precious, each with its colour and shape. I will lie on my back and watch the cloudshapes float by, puzzle how and why the dog should turn into a camel and the light shines through the shapes till the earth is a flat surface on which I begin to spin, lying flat on my back with blades of grass prickling my earlobes, tickling the backs of my knees, I see how the clouds move and the earth begins to move beneath me and now my head begins to spin until there is neither above nor below and all things are moving, swiftly, without sound, and I am falling, falling into the clear blue, freely in space. Now the door opens. Soon I will be outside, in pools of shadow under the trees, drops of water still hang on the grasses, gleam cool on the cobwebs by the woodshed, under the eaves. It is still early, fresh and cool in the ebbtide of night, the shadows guard their secrets for me to find. The morning is long. Now the sun is only just touching the far end of the garden, where leaves move in a dazzle of light. The rest lies in a pool of blue shadow. It is only just beginning.

2

I am running through empty streets. The sky is black and
without stars. All my life I have been running, down the
dark underside. Now I am exposed, and all doors are
locked. The house fronts turn me away, blind cold stone.
I try to conceal myself in a doorway, but it is too shallow,
the shadow falls on my stark white body as the moon
rises above the sloping rooftops, the shadowed chimney
stacks, and already cold bluish light falls on my curved
breasts, thighs and crotch. A bush of dark hair grows
between my legs, I put my hand across it, the other arm
across my two heavy breasts, but the doorway is too
narrow, I am clearly visible in the doorway, shivering as
much with shame as the cold night air which touches my
exposed shoulders, buttocks and shrinking belly. I know
that my situation, for which I am not responsible, since
I do not know how I came to be here, is hopeless; also,

that I am somehow to blame. Behind closed shutters, round the corners of these silent streets, dark and narrow, lurk the prowling night wolves whose one desire is to mock and frighten. Shuddering, I wait. Footsteps are heard, but fade into silence. Nobody comes. I would give my soul for a strip of cloth to wrap round myself.

I have been prowling these night cities for ages. Night after night I have been running, and will continue to run, into the future. As a child I was pursued by a witch who gave chase, will o' the wisps danced in the dark above us both until she had me, popped me into her conjuror's box and, after only a touch of her ebony wand, transformed me, one two hullaballoo, into a fluttering brown bird with panicky wings. Just as I knew she would. And then the night was a jungle through which prowled an all-knowing tiger, he was coming for me, even if I stayed indoors, hid under the bedclothes, he would sniff me out through the cracks in the window, peer through a gap in the drawn blinds and find me out.

The night is my own. I walk barefoot to the window and draw back the curtains. I watch moonlight over the silent gardens, shadows sucked into the apple tree like ink into blotting paper. Nobody watches me, nobody hears. A black cat slinks noiselessly over the roof of the garden shed and vanishes into the shadows. The moonlight throws shadows on the wall, the sloping bars of the window run across my body. I move to my body, dance to my moving shadow, I am a prima ballerina, Desdemona pleading for her life, see how she stretches out her arms, how the shadow of her long hair falls on her falling nightgown, I never did offend you in my life. There

16

are few words, but the images come crowding through the shadows thrown by the moon. Now it is a white horse and rider moving through the forest, the moon drifts upward on a bank of drifting luminous cloud, is shut out by the closing treetops through which the wind sighs as it runs through the leaves at the bottom of the garden now quite dark, his hooves find moss, small grey boulders, flowers bloom as in a medieval tapestry on the forest floor. He is moving towards her, she knows it but he does not, though he weaves through trees tall as masts as a lodestone pulled towards its star, and for him to find her it is necessary for her to be rooted to the spot, arranged on a bank of moss, looking touchingly helpless in her thin white gown with the dark tresses falling about her graceful shoulders. Why? My ankle, she says, smiling weakly, I have been in this place for several hours. And because I am almost insensible with fatigue and lack of food I am allowed to sink back, enjoy the delicious sensation of his strong arms round my body. I close my eyes. He lifts me up onto the front of his horse. And then what? I wait. Nothing happens. The film on the screen of my eyelids has stopped moving forward, and I am frowning into empty black.

The house is steeped in moonlight and sleep. No sound from beyond the wall. I am safe. Now is the time when neither of them can harm me. Now is the time when I come out of my disguise, tiptoe through the shadowed room and draw back the curtains, watch the luminous night outside. The moon drifts swiftly through banks of cloud which drift, black with unspent rage in the middle but otherwise bright with eerie light. All things have been changed. I am changed. Outside the ugly little gardens with their small-minded fences and petty lawns have become one huge mystery, dark and joyous. The dark bank of trees which, in daylight, hardly screens this house from its neighbours, is drenched in night, has sucked up shadows and now whispers secrets to the cool night air. It is alive, it sighs with a sudden gust of wind and has become a wood. I hear an owl hoot. Now I am free, the road is swallowed in shadow, silent now, to affirm my freedom I dance round the centre of my room, take huge leaps, careful, however, to land quietly on the patterned carpet. I am an insect with unused wings just come out of a husk. I have to stretch them because they are crumpled. I feel myself move, such freedom, how the air touches my bare skin under the loose gown, now I open a window to feel more, cold air blows on my throat, through my loose hair, now the nightmare has blown into the shadows, out of sight. My cocoon lies, folded neatly on a chair, underwear, stockings, hooks and elastic, but even without them she would see to it that I do not move freely. I have only to do something, lift, bend, reach for, and she will pull me up short. Not nice, unladylike, or words to suggest my body has become indecent, to be strapped in, hidden from prying eyes. I do not know what I have done wrong, only that I must be ashamed, and that my body has odours which will turn milk sour.

What a child I was, in the old days. Lying in bed I pulled at my nipples, looked anxiously for signs of some small swelling. I was in such a hurry, to grow, begin the change. And now I am strapped in, covered, I walk down the road in my school uniform stiff as a ramrod, my knees close together, conscious of the bloodstained pad rubbing the skin which is tender on the inside of my thighs, glancing fearfully behind in case tell-tale marks show on the back of my skirt.

But now, in the dark, I enter my secret world. Through the open window I see trees stand deep in shadow, while the small fringed lawn gleams vacant under a rising moon. Now the deckchairs are all stacked out of sight, and the dreadful small talk heard above the tinkle of teaspoons and cups. Folded, stacked up for the night, those stupid chattering adults.

Now nobody can see me. They watch me, through each hour of the day. I have a torch, so I can read my books undisturbed, but I let it lie in the desk drawer. They do not want me to escape, that is why they spy on me through each hour of the day, why I am not permitted to shut myself in my room, why I am told that reading is bad for my eyes, why they stand on the doorstep when I come back late, the reason why she always finds something for me to do, dishes to wash, dusting, some foolish ritual like place mats on the polished oak table, or I must sit stiffly on the end of the sofa, hair brushed, knees tight together, and say yes, no, pretend to listen to their boring talk, smile politely for visitors while all I want to do through the tedious hours is to escape, shut myself up in this room, shut out the sound of their silly voices, drown the sound in a surge of music which sets my pulse racing, how the solo violin lifts upward, upward like a bird ascending, now it takes me with it, flying up, up, I did not know it was possible for pure sound to do so much, more than words, now I have escaped: I am pure spirit, I follow the sound like a pattern embedded deep in my head, inevitable as my own blood moving, the sound is now my own blood flowing, my pulse throbbing, the sound of my own soul crying out. With rage, passion, but also a terrible joy.

Leaning out of the window, I feel how the cool night air touches my face and bare shoulders; how it gathers in the shadows of the trees, stirring the leaves which sigh as it moves on; how it shakes perfume out of the ghostly bush of jasmine below me, and now drifts up; how it moves the moving shadows of clouds made luminous by a drifting moon. Standing like this, undisturbed, with nobody to see me, I know that I could be part of this whole thing, music and words, the entire universe, if only they would let me be. Because the world which they have chosen to inhabit, and in which I stand awkwardly on the sidelines, sulky and self-conscious, is anyhow false. How stupid, I say aloud, laughing into the dark. They do not know, cannot hear, but meanwhile they hold me trapped in this unhappy house, sitting silent at the oak table as I have been told to do, back erect, hands on the table, but never elbows, I pass the gravy boat from him to her, potato bowl from her to him, the salt cellar to each in turn without an extra word having been spoken, because one word could cause an explosion, I sit between them, she is white-faced and tight-lipped, he frowning, sitting hunched over the plate, and all I want is to be allowed to leave the table, to shut myself in this room, out of range of their hatred which crackles ominously like an electric storm and could, probably will erupt round me, the lightning conductor. It is no use, it does not matter how often I stack the dishes, set place mats and cutlery, peel potatoes or wash up, the problem of my being in this house is unresolved, since it has nothing to do with my behaviour or the number of unwashed dishes but with them, their rage and resentment with what they feel for each other, with the stupid lives they have somehow constructed in and around each other. And since I am the focus, since all this goes on night and day in this stuffy little house which is like a prison, a house in which each word is audible through the walls, in which each person moves through furniture which must be dusted, eats without appetite through meals which have to be cooked, from plates which must be stacked, washed and put away yet again, speaks to someone who must be heard, deferred to, pecked on the cheek as though in love, since all this is endured in the name of family, duty, it follows that they resent me bitterly. Nothing I do is right, nothing can, nothing could ever be enough. I have been taught to say 'Can I do anything?' as a kind of apology for her domestic martyrdom, but I know there is nothing I can do. There could never be enough furniture to dust, silver to polish, or unnecessary chores to propitiate her rage. Worst of all, I am not conscious of gratitude for their wasted and tormented lives.

It is only at night, now, standing at the window with a calm moon drifting silently above the dark gardens, now so soothingly peaceful that I can feel the true freedom of growing, becoming, which makes life so exciting now that I can hear music, read words with new meanings, something so thrilling that my whole body is tense as a strung bow, I must find release in dance, movement, and I watch the shadow of my arm on the moonlit wall and admire its grace. That is the curious thing, even while in sleep my body turns to nightmare, while the clothes she forces me to wear are hideous and I cannot bend, stretch or lift without a reproof to remind me of my indecency, some secret vice which has somehow become inherent to me, like sweat in my armpits (she sews waterproof pads into cotton frocks) or the white stains in my underwear, even while this is so, in my secret room I exult in the way my breasts have grown like those of an adult, the curve of my hips gives me pleasure, I study the line of neck and shoulder as though it belonged to somebody else, and as though it was somebody else looking back at me from the mirror I appraise the line of her chin and the smooth white forehead above winged eyebrows and those remarkable eyes which look back at me so seriously. So this is she, I say, watching the apparition. And sometimes, standing under the apple tree in my pale blue dress, one hand resting lightly on the rough dark bark, I say to the world of the empty garden and the houses beyond: this is she, here I am. And once this spring, coming out of the woodshed the sun dazzled me, I had to bend down or the untrimmed pale boughs bright with yellow forsythia would have tangled in my dark hair as it grew above the woodshed door, and I stood blinking into the bright light and the voice inside me said: Here I am, here she is, the young woman with blossoms round her head, look how she stands. I am standing on the threshold of my life.

But how long must I wait for it to begin, how long before I escape from this house? I am trapped in it, the

furniture that needs dusting, the sour twist of her mouth
and the talk which is always small and increasingly bitter.
I listen, but all is quiet through the wall. I wish I had
a lock on my door. If only they would leave me alone,
with these books, my journal and the sounds that come
out of the radio. But a voice calls up the small staircase:
What are you doing up there? Come down and say hello
to the visitors, and I sit on a chair while they glance at
me occasionally, the child who has grown suddenly, who
does not seem to know what to do with herself, not saying
a word but slouching forward in her chair, watching the
faces move as they make small talk from under her long
drooping hair. My mother smiles. Neither fish nor flesh
she says, meaning me. I do not know what it signifies,
but she likes to put a label, some sort of category on my
behaviour and what it represents, she is oddly smug and
confident as she brings out the words. What are you
talking about? I asked, standing on the landing outside my
door. It means, she told me, that you are neither one thing
nor the other. I shrugged. I do not mind what she says, or
thinks. It means nothing, if it makes her content I am glad.
But when she went through my things and read my journal,
told me so, laughing in my face, I could have throttled her
on the spot to stop the words from coming out.

I listen, but all is quiet through the wall. Soon a new
day will begin. The seasons have begun to follow each
other with alarming speed. I remember last spring,
when the first crocuses pushed through the meagre grass
under the apple tree and I had my birthday. Another
year of my life. Soon I will leave school, I can count
the years on the fingers of one hand, and I know how

quickly they will go by. Because I remember not only last winter, subdued mornings when thick white fog curled like an animal rubbing its back against the window glass, mornings when trees appeared like ghosts through a thin veil of mist on the walk to school, but the winter before which was hard, for weeks the garden lay under several feet of snow, its surface turned hard as glass with black specks visible amidst solidified footprints to the woodshed, we slid in the playground and outside in the road before men arrived in a lorry to scatter grit, and the footpath to the front door had to be attacked with a spade. One winter, two. Nights closing in, dark mornings. Followed by spring, crocuses breaking through under the apple tree, blossom breaking and falling, breaking to fall yet again the following year, blow in drifts along the road. I count the years now, each spring another birthday. I count the years of my life adding up. I have hardly begun to live, but soon I will be old.

But when I was small, only a few years ago, I would count the seconds, knowing the huge expanse of a single minute, and that this vastness had to be multiplied as many times for a single hour. As for tomorrow, it was inconceivable. Nobody could be expected to wait until tomorrow. And everything had colour, colour and light. I woke to the sound of the cock crowing in the house by the sea and the sun was already spilling into the room, making a bright pool on the bare wood floor. Each day was summer, hot, endless, nothing could stop the sun rising in the same slow arc through the same blue sky, travelling constant above my head, days like a string of clear glass beads, or the soap bubbles which I blew from my clay pipe, shining as they floated upward, holding the colour of all things, trees and grass and sky in a tenuous circle of light. And the two of them young, playful, on holiday, wearing loose white clothes and moving quickly, with ease, the sound of their voices murmuring, but also laughing through the thin wall. Shrieks, and the ringing sound of laughter from the far side of the garden in the sleepy shadow of afternoon.

Now they are changed. The moon has sunk below the line of trees. The sky begins to fade. Soon a fresh day will have begun, I will hear a groan through the wall, bedsprings and the sound of him clearing catarrh from his throat as he does each morning, clearing his nasal passages over the washbasin in the bathroom before he gargles. How it disgusts me, his gross body making loud noises through the wall, the flabby paunch and white skin as he crosses the landing wearing only pyjama pants, the feel of his unshaved chin when he plants his morning kiss on my face, scratching bristle, bad breath smelling foul, her face mud-coloured, the eyes flat, still lifeless with unbrushed hair showing streaks of grey. I want to close my eyes and ears, so that I cannot see, hear or smell, thick walls to shut out all sounds and give me privacy. A world of my own, allowing in only what is beautiful: music, books, moonlight riding the dark shadows across ghostly lawns and the dying breath of high trees, my own haunting image in the murky mirror.

I confront the shadow which looks out at me from the oval mirror. Who are you, I whisper, coming forward so close to the surface that her dark solemn eyes gaze with alarming gravity at me. I study the fine line of her brows, which sweep upward, then taper down like the wings of a bird in flight. Pushing back the falling hair I study the shape of the smooth white brow and find it passable, but the nose disturbs me, for the hundredth time I push my forefinger against its fleshy base and press upward, turning my head to the side I reaffirm that such a minor change would remove my only grievance, but as yet long periods of pressure have only produced pain at the base without changing its shape. I find it ironic that such a minor alteration could mean so much and still remain out of reach. But time is on my side, I will keep trying. I step back and the dark hair falls to the shoulders, delicate curves, thin arms, how the small face gleams in the dark, ivory pale, those two dark eyes stare back. Who are you? I whisper, and the solemn eyes stare back without a word. Sometimes I have felt their strange power turned on others, adults, those in authority. Now I turn it on men. I do not know why I, or rather she, since I do not feel completely one and the same person on such occasions, should do this, or want to. But I have felt how her solemn dark eyes have stared into the back of men's heads until they turned, transfixed, how one man's eyes in particular will always find hers, across the crowded assembly hall during morning prayers, behind her desk in the schoolroom, even out of doors during sports day, I have only to watch and his eyes will find me, one among many he will find me out, as though such eyes could burn, transmit wordless messages of some sort. I am frightened of it, this curious magnetism, once I felt his eyes watching me during a sudden downpour, a group stood waiting under cover looking on as tall trees

26

dripped water, nobody broke the silence as wind stirred the high branches and raindrops pattered drily on a brittle flood of old leaves on the ground, I knew he was watching me, for a long time I would not turn my head, pretending not to be aware I looked down at a patch of dark green moss near my foot, when at last I did turn my head to answer his black gaze it was with a kind of triumph. What do you want, I asked in my look. For once I was not frightened, quite cool, free of the hot burning flush rising in my body, the hammer under my ribcage was still. Now, just for a second, I was in control. Afterwards, when the sun had come through the branches and the group moved forward, forming new patterns, talking, I stayed behind, with him, staring down at the mound of soft moss close to my foot, though I chattered as gaily as the rest. Both of us did. I keep going over the scene in my mind, night after night. I close my eyes in the dark, rain falls through the cool wood. Standing with my back to the wall of the shelter I wait for the moment when I will turn my head.

She laughed at me, when I told her, but in spite of everything I am not a child. I hide my diary in the underwear drawer where she will not find it easily. I wish I had a lock on my door, since she does not regard me as somebody with a right to privacy. How dare she mock me, if I feel such pain. I know that it is absurd, since nothing can bridge the gap between us, he being old now, so old that I could never catch up. Last night I wrote in my diary, 'I do not want to forget, ever, what it feels like to be me now.' That is why I keep writing things down. I am changing, I know that. I will continue to change, and some day I will be old, a woman like my mother. Except that I do not want to turn into somebody like her, that is why I write it down, to remind myself, how it was, how it is now, everything so intense, nothing absurd or childlike, it hurts, but then again how wonderful the world is now, how sharply I see colours, the shapes of things, the sky now turning pink and gold above the dark line of trees, feel my body moving, hair lightly touching my shoulders, cool air running down smooth skin, a tingling sensation going through me as cold air comes in from the window, giving me goose pimples, and I watch small hairs rising on my arm, hear birds singing sleepily now in the shadow of the apple tree. The brown skin of my arm smells of summer afternoons spent lying on the edge of a cricket field with a book. Discussing it: life. Chewing a grass stem for the sweet crunch between my teeth. Revising French verbs and thinking how life, like a dome of many-coloured glass, stains the white radiance. As we lie, books forgotten, grass tickling the backs of our knees, squinting into the sunlight and feeling how the world revolves under our backs as the clouds move overhead, till everything is spinning and I close my eyes against the bright sunlight and feel how my lids become a burning membrane, the colour of my own blood, through which everything floods in, the sound of a high slow aeroplane droning overhead, the smell of dry grass and baked earth, of my baked forearm lying across my mouth, and coming years spinning ahead, nebulous as clouds, drifting in curious shapes. How it is now.

3

Grey light coming from the gap in the curtains. Perhaps it is still early. I sleep so badly now, to wake in the small hours. No sounds through the wall, thank god, I can lie in the gloom and stare at the stained wallpaper. No hope of real rest, deep sleep eludes me even though I am always tired. Night is a choppy, murky ocean, dreams disturb it, indistinct shadows with no outline, now I am tossed up on the muddy foreshore like a stranded whale. Lying on my back, I shall never stand upright, not without a helping hand.

Lying on my back, pinned down by the weight in my distended belly, I would like to laugh aloud. You up there, looking up at the ceiling which is not as white as it ought to be, the crack has come through again and I still have not reached the strand of grey cobweb blowing in the far corner, you god, whatever you call yourself, have certainly used me for your own purposes. I have known that from the first moment, after you had reached down and seized me in your huge hand, squeezed me like a rubber ball and left me gasping. It was no use screaming, you were deaf. The hand simply came back, grasped me firmly round the middle and crushed me for the thing I was, simply a pod, an envelope. To be torn up, used. Not the person I was so proud to be, so carefully cherished, nurtured through the growing years, a unique structure defined by high walls of emotion, shelves of intellect stacked with a whole armoury of definitions, constructs, the lofty roofbeam hung with colourful ideals, their fine silk stirring with each wind that blew. Within five minutes of my coming into that room, cream walls, high bed, bloodstains on the floor from the previous victim, the whole structure had come tumbling down, just like a child's building bricks scattered on the floor. In the interim between screaming to deaf walls, unable to get down from the hard high bed placed like a sacrificial altar, I thought: So this is what it's all about, I am not a person but a pod, to be used and prised open, nothing but a tool for some huge blind force.

I lie on my back, which aches. Cold air comes from the window, but I feel hot and flushed. It is a struggle to lie on my side, and when I do I almost always feel worse. So I do not attempt to move, not yet. Each time I take a breath I feel a hot wave running under my skin. I kick back the sheet and look down at the huge bulge which my belly has become. I cannot see my crotch, have not had a glimpse of it for several weeks. Even my legs have become remote. I find it curious to be out of communion with half my body. As I perform the most ordinary functions, wash and dress, walk with unusual caution down the staircase carrying cups, I have to take my feet on trust, assume the bottom half is doing out of habit what I am unable to oversee. Anything that drops on the floor is out of reach, I see it from a great height and sigh, knowing that to bend forward involves a dangerous loss of equilibrium. A huge mass of fluid, flesh and bone will pull me down.

Judging from the light now visible from the window it is going to be another cloudy day, the sky a solid bank of grey cloud. It has been a depressing summer so far, but now I am glad of it. One small movement, the slightest exertion, makes me hot and sweaty. I have been up several times during the night, now I lie tired but wide awake. The child had a bad dream and woke crying in wet sheets, but this one is far more impatient, he kicked and stirred several times in the dark while I lay, my head confused by the last dream, and felt what he did.

Looking down, my belly is curiously lopsided. I run my fingers along the hard bulge, back and cranium, till the taut skin gives way to flesh that is soft and malleable. He turns turtle, this one, like a subaquatic gymnast, several times a day. Sometimes I wake to find him lying across me, feet sticking out one side, head the other, or his weight pressing hard up against my ribcage. On mornings when his skull presses up into my stomach I still feel nausea. For months I have been finicky about food.

If only there was not so much to do, I could perhaps doze off after lunch. If the child is good, and sleeps too.

I lumber through the day like a great clumsy elephant, doing small things, so many jobs which need to be done. Once I have pushed the child in her pushchair, a bag of groceries and my own weight up the hill from the shops, I am done for, I could collapse and doze off for several hours. But my eyes and ears are tied, the whole of my body is at the service of a thousand small things, the child runs on unsteady legs while I watch in case she tumbles, listen as much for silence as a sudden cry, clean up the mess she makes, brush and bathe, fasten shoe buckles before our walk in the park, sit by her for hours with spoon poised till she opens her mouth or spits it out, scrape the food I have prepared from her chin, add the plate to the unwashed pile in the sink, stained bib to the heap of soiled garments in the bathroom. I leave her for an hour while the doctor takes my blood pressure, listens to the small heart beating in my belly, lays the flat of his hands on my belly as though moulding a new human being into shape, and says everything is fine. In the corridor I sit in a line of heavy women, all waiting for their time. How long to go, each asks of the one next in line, when are you due?

I try not to think, or if, then only about the next half hour. My mind is stupid now, slow as my body, it has stopped racing ahead, into the future. Just let me get through the day. Perhaps, before nightfall, I will be lying on a high table between four white walls, in the grip of a scream I cannot control. No. No. Try not to think ahead. And yet I wish it had begun, so does he from the feel of him. From where I lie I can see the small suitcase standing in the corner by the dressing table. It has stood ready for weeks, according to instructions. But I do not think it will be today. These last few weeks have been slow, endlessly slow. The minutes drag, as the hours now drag, each long day as heavy as my body. Time swells, as I do, a hanging drop of water on a branch, growing larger, round and heavy: if only it would fall. If only the thin membrane would break at long last, under the pressure.

I try not to think. I dare not think too far ahead. Then my pulse begins to race, I feel slightly sick, weak tears prick in my eyes. What is the point, I am trapped for life, so heavy I need a helping hand to haul me upright. And once he is born, then what, perhaps I will get my old shape back, look as slim as I did before, but for what, what is the use, I shall be doubly trapped, two mouths crying for food, mummy, two helpless beings who turn to me, relying on my good will, my submission. I have no future, not now. Nothing lies ahead but this.

I listen, but no sound comes through the wall. She cried in the dark, during the small hours, and the sound broke through the thin walls of my sleep. I am alert within seconds nowadays. How quickly she went under, once I had touched her, made her comfortable, murmured the usual soothing words and tucked her in. I saw the heavy lids drop, her face grow smooth and still. Now she will perhaps sleep an extra hour. I count these rare moments of quiet and solitude.

He lies with his back turned to me, not stirring. He did not move when the child cried in the night, when I switched on the reading lamp for a while, or got up to go to the bathroom. Unable to doze off, escape from this cumbersome body, the weight of fluid, pressure on the bladder, gurgling sounds of an underground sea stirring under the dark caves of my ribs, and him leaping like a live fish as he turns and kicks. Unable to escape from my own thinking head I heard the minutes ticking away and watched the ring of light thrown into the shadows of the ceiling.

All through the night he showed no sign, lying rigid, still as a rock. Sometimes I have a suspicion that he lies too still, unwilling to show he is conscious. But I know he sleeps soundly. It is as though nothing will crack his composure. He sleeps soundly, knowing for sure that I will get up if the child wakes. He has not heard her cry since the night she was born. And if I should begin to cry he will turn deaf, will turn his back however loud I shout, throw things, he will walk through the door and not come back. That's right, he says, turn on the water-works, as though I could, perform such agony.

I look towards his form outlined under the bedclothes. Light from the window catches his rumpled dark hair, his body is a hard cliff. The waves of my misery beat hopelessly into that rock, to fall back on itself. Nothing is allowed to crack his composure. He will not hear, he will not see. It is impossible to discuss what could be wrong. He surrounds himself in silence, across this room stands a wall built block by block of things left in the air, not put into words. If I try to shout, it grows bigger as he adds another layer. If I push, he vanishes through the door.

That is it, I am bound. This house is my prison. I am bound by my body, its fruit, growing inside and out.

Somehow he wants to hurt me through this, knowing it. When he walks through the door he is saying: I can go, the one thing you are unable to do. He wants me to know something, by staying out all night, even though he refuses to speak. He wants to hurt, to insult me by his behaviour.

I do not understand what is happening. The harder I try, the more aloof he seems to become. It is not as though I have done anything terrible. On the contrary, I think I have improved. I have become skilful, know how to cope with far more, and I do not ask for much, hardly anything now. I have learnt to manage by myself, since I have to anyhow. Once he used to give so much, constantly, without being asked. He worked so hard for us both, to get this house, clean it up. We planned spaces, colour schemes, where to build bookcases; he bought gallons of paint, stood on ladders, while I sewed curtains. It was so much fun, being able to plan and arrange our own rooms for the first time, leave lodgings behind. Our own bathroom, snugly shut in behind our own front door.

The child kicks. Cold air blows through the window, lifting the edge of the curtain. Outside a glimpse of sullen sky, grey and heavy. The body in the neighbouring bed stirs slightly, coughs, snuffles, and is still. Through the wall a subdued thud, a slight squeak as the motion of the child's body causes the cot castors to slide across the linoleum and collide with the skirting. But no cry. In the quiet street below, the sound of milk bottles being put on the step. Footsteps on gravel, a shudder and rattle of glass in crates, it moves on a few yards, stops, moves forward and out of earshot till tomorrow morning. Each day is much like the last, with the steady rhythm of the milkman working his way down the road from house to house. It will continue, day after long day.

I have no alternative but to suppose that it will continue. Everything I have, everything I value is wrapped round the child now asleep in the next room. As though that was not bad enough, my life blood is now running into a second who will hold me hostage to fortune if the first could not do it. I cannot see a way ahead except to continue, hour by hour, day following day, trying hard not to mind, trying not to let it show, at least during the hours of daylight. Once shadows and evening silence slant across the house, once I sit alone in a room, I struggle with misery.

It is quite incomprehensible. If he knows why, he will not say. That is the worst thing, not knowing why. He was the one who wanted to marry, who found this house, who arranged everything so that it should turn out this way. Except for the child. And yet he seems fond of it now.

I ought to get up. So much to do, small jobs, chores I left last night because I was tired. I am constantly tired nowadays, but I suppose it is to be expected. My breasts have grown heavy, swollen, aureoles like pale brown moons. When I touch them, sticky yellow fluid comes from the nipples, I see each enlarged pore from which the milk will be sucked. Now I have a moment to ask myself: am I the person I used to be before all this? I am an animal, bound by the cries of the flesh, tenderness, anxiety, each in turn, and beyond this a whole network of small domestic duties which comprise and are bound to such feeling. But I have not changed: I only see quite clearly that my life now makes demands which must be met.

But he seems to have withdrawn, unwilling to become responsible. He is resentful, and if he is cold, deceitful, giving no reason for his changed behaviour, he is trying to hurt, as though saying, do it on your own. And I must, I lumber heavily, clumsily, bumping into furniture, the passage and doorways difficult and narrow. I pick up things, trying not to drop them because I cannot reach the floor. I fight lack of appetite and swallow what is required to build healthy bones and tissue. I breathe as instructed, lying flat on my back, lifting each leg in turn, slowly. I do not allow the child to watch me cry.

I have learnt to live among small things. The shape of a vase standing on the window sill. The fresh smell of stiff white cloth when I gather in the day's wash from the line outside and fold it into my basket. Gossip on a bench in the park. Finishing off a knitted garment into which she will grow. Next month. The thread running through my fingers, the steady texture being shaped as I count stitches under my breath keeps me stable. She runs after a ball on the grass, stumbles and falls. For a brief moment she is undecided whether or not to cry. She picks herself up and continues. Yesterday her face would have continued to pucker, she would have stood rooted, shrieked until I came for her. The thread of wool continues to run through my fingers: the child grows, my body grows, the wool coat grows under my fingers. I count days, hours, stitches. There is nothing beyond, no thoughts, or dreams. I want grey walls in our living room. I have decided. And sunshine yellow curtains since the room faces north. Today the child spoke a word I have not heard before. The foetus is now head down, and feels lower. I have finished the second sleeve.

I am committed, hour after hour, day after day. Once I would not have thought it credible, but it is so. I do not read much: by the time the child is settled down for the night, the dishes washed and stacked, I feel too exhausted. My mind is numb, the words say nothing. I have nothing to say. I have just enough time to knit the collar before going to bed. Tomorrow I will stitch the seams, perhaps first press the separate pieces under a damp cloth. I count the housekeeping money in my purse. I calculate how much a child's wool coat would have cost ready-made, how much money I have saved. But it is not just to save that I do it. It is tangible, under my fingers, how time has gone by, each stitch a second, holding my life in a border of moss stitch pattern, a shape, something to show for it.

In the child's room are several drawers full of such clothes. Some have been washed so many times they have lost all their colour and shape; those outgrown stored for the unborn. I began with intricate patterns, shell shapes, lace made with fine needles and thin wool which took hours of solitude with the dusk falling, no sound of the key turning in the front door, long after the lamp was lit. Now I knit thick and plain to keep up with larger sizes. I am impatient of delicate work, which is fragile and useless.

Looking ahead, through the half-open door, I can see

the pattern of my day spread out. It is tied to the walls
of this house, to the floors and windows, to objects such
as milk bottles and saucepans, blankets, spoons and
small shoes which need to be buckled regularly. I do not
know who I am, amongst all this. I wash, scrape, fasten,
while all surfaces collect not so much dust as brightly
coloured objects of wood and plastic. Building bricks
which have tumbled, a wooden horse and a small cart
make the floor an obstacle course which, by the end of
each day, must be laboriously picked up and put away.
The sound in my head is of nursery jingles, I have begun
once more with the alphabet, simple words, round red
apples, rabbits who wear pinafores. We thrive on repeti-
tion, she and I, the same words for a bedtime story, for
spoonfuls of food coaxed into her mouth, for getting
through the day with a minimum of anguish. During
daylight hours everything is excluded except these things,
soiled clothes and pictures at the bottom of the plate.
Even after dusk it is hard to see beyond this, since the
following day will be much the same, the quiet evening
only a respite which could be broken at any moment
by a cry. Tomorrow I shall have to find new shoes, a
size larger; she will say several new words.

I can hear sounds through the wall. She is talking to
herself in a singsong voice. I must move, before those
contented sounds become shrill, demanding. But now I
smile, hearing how she wakes each morning, those soft
sounds, lilting, I have never been able to make out the
words. Perhaps she counts flowers on the wallpaper along
the wall by her cot, as I did, hour after hour. It seemed
like hours, anyhow. But it sounds more like a story, as

though she was telling herself something soothing. The sound of her voice is as soft as her flesh, the plump rings round her wrists. It comes with a slight shock of surprise to know that this small person in privacy, with the door of her room closed, lives in her own world.

My life is clearly marked out now. When the child is fifteen I shall be forty. When she is a woman of twenty-five I will be fifty, the age of my mother. I worked it out in the hospital ward a few hours after she was born. Nil, twenty-five, fifty, in a recurring pattern, I could not get over the fact, or that it had not occurred to me before. Once it had occurred to me it was as though the time was already spent in advance, everything I am reduced to numbers, as though after this birth the years would go tick tock like a clock mechanism, the year of walking, tick, the year of talking, tock, now it is time to go to school, tick tock, her milk teeth must be pulled, school reports considered, also music lessons, but what, amongst all this of the person I wished to become, will she be pushed into the background, to emerge like a spectre from behind mirrors, stir like a whisper in the space between books, hover over my shoulder as I sit slumped in a chair with a child falling asleep, a feeding bottle still in its mouth, to cause mayhem after nightfall, an angry poltergeist who throws cups at the walls, growls for food and drink, bangs doors and shrieks in a frantic bid for attention and, sobbing, wakes the household? The ghost is in the room now, I can feel it moving uneasily towards the second bed, hesitant whether to go forward and touch the head with its fingers. It always comes at dusk to watch him come through the door, stands rigid and pale, for hours if need be, while lamps are lit, the sky beyond the window loses its final light and the house fills with shadows. If he does not come it stands guard all night, warding off both sleep and dreams. Perhaps it will fade from sheer weariness, or it could, after days, perhaps weeks of quietude, cause sudden and violent havoc. I simply do not know.

I live by the hour now, and I want to carry my responsibility gladly, lightly. Since it has grown from my own body. I want to sing over the washtub, look up into the sky and watch a lark glide just for a moment as I remove pegs from the line and bundle the sweet-smelling cotton sheets into my arms, I want the rooms filled with sunlight, to move between walls glowing back in shades of sienna, old rose and myosotis blue, to walk through doorways gleaming with white paint towards windows where plants grow into outside daylight, I want the spaces between such walls to be filled with contentment, fresh air, the subdued sounds of laughter and music, and love. I do not understand what has happened to it, I have taken it for granted, thought it as natural as leaves growing on a tree, cannot think why it has been withdrawn. I live from hour to hour, since I must. Hush, I say to the ghost which glides through the shadowy rooms after nightfall, my child is asleep upstairs. Do not disturb things. But my terror is such that I tremble, and sometimes I find it possible to cry.

He stirs in the other bed, mumbles something under his breath into the pillow. I do not know what he is saying. Soon the alarm clock will go off, but he needs me to shake him by the shoulder, draw back the curtains and lumber cautiously down to the kitchen to fill the kettle and prepare tea. I slide each foot step by step, pulling my dressing-gown tight, but even so I cannot see where I am going. I grasp the banister, fearful of a fall. I will come back and shake his slack body in the second bed, since he is slow, perhaps reluctant to wake fully. In the grey light of this cloudy overcast morning I will see how the skin of his face is creased from folds in the bedclothes, imprinted, how flushed and puffy it looks. He sleeps like somebody who has been drugged, as though he was sick; only after I have come back with a thick mug of steaming tea, placed it beside the alarm clock and called his name, firmly shaking him by the shoulder, does he respond enough to lift himself up from the bedclothes and, propped on an elbow, drinks from the thick white mug ringed with blue lines. His eyelids are drooping, veiled in steam. I do not know this man, nor does he recognize me. He has been somewhere else, at the bottom of some disturbed murky ocean. But I sleep lightly, riding currents of black air like a bird or leaf. I am fully awake in a second.

I am constantly restless. Through the wall the child has stopped babbling. Perhaps she has dozed off, or something has caught her attention. The hours ahead are full of tasks, my body is slow now, but I am almost feverish to do too much. Not enough time. From down the road I can make out the shrill sound of the workmen's drill. An old house nearby is being demolished, pushing the child each day I see the hole in the road, old interiors briefly exposed, the worn lining of faded private lives open to the sky, then crumble to dust and rubble. I think of the old man who would have coloured that patch of wall, the surface round the torn hearth, now ripped out, with such painstaking hope. So much to do. Most of my life still lies ahead. So much I want to see, and do. I know the crumbling wall, its flaking skins, are a warning. But I am trapped in such walls, and do not know how to get out. I should not be thinking only of old rose, sienna or myosotis blue like sky. I should be finding a way out. But I see nothing ahead, only the possibility of an abyss I must cross.

Meanwhile I live from day to day, coping with each thing as it comes, within the narrow confines of each day. Perhaps it will all change after the child is born, for better or worse, though I cannot think how. I must move through the heavy hours with as much patience as I can summon up, wearily, weighed down with the future, it hangs in my belly like a drop of water which grows large on a branch and refuses to fall. I would shake it if I could. Yesterday I climbed on a stepladder and washed down the kitchen paintwork, but felt nothing. Perhaps today I will clean down the bathroom walls. But I know I can do nothing, I am in this prison until something decides it is ready, the time is ripe. Then the membrane breaks, the swollen drop falls from the branch. Who decides: the child kicking and turning in the dark of his underground sea? Folklore would have it so, to hear doctors and nurses speak of it down at the clinic. But I doubt it, though I like to think it too, feeling him move and kick inside me, knowing the rapid sound of his heart heard through a stethoscope through a background of ocean noises, communing with my hand laid flat on the skin of my belly now. I do not know. Perhaps he is as much a prisoner, doing time in my body, until something decides, or the membrane breaks under the weight of water and it begins. I do not know, nobody does.

The child is alert now, and hungry. She has begun to screech quite seriously, calling my name. The cot thuds against the wall, bump, bump, as she bounces up and down on the mattress. My day has begun. I must feed her, change her, make breakfast. I will move from room to room, carrying things, pull back the sheets, open windows to let in fresh air, strap the child in her pushchair and walk down the hill with dust rising and the sound of the pneumatic drill thudding through my body as we pass the roadworks, attend to the price and colour of vegetables, fruit, choose and buy, push the child, my body, leaning wearily forward, slowly up the hill with the extra weight of a full shopping bag, stopping to talk to the child, pausing for breath occasionally, I will notice how the old house now being pulled down still has one high wall upright, above the first floor level it was painted a brave blue by somebody who attempted to create a home that would last, and now look, how it is exposed to the sky, the cold stares of just anybody, how shabby it looks now, with a scar where the hearth has been ripped out and old wallpaper ending in sky and a heap of rubble. What has become of the person who chose that shade of blue, has he picked himself up or is he down in the rubble, a discarded bundle of old rags? I watch the house, which is like our house, coming down under a summer sky. Perhaps today or tomorrow it will have vanished, just so much rubble. It disturbs me, how quickly things alter, how little value is placed on things. But I must keep moving, try not to think to no purpose. I will come back, unpack my shopping bag, and prepare lunch. If she sleeps for an hour I will put my feet up as instructed, watching the sky from the window, how it constantly changes, how clouds move, light turns from grey to silver and back to a darker grey, how heavy rainclouds change shape, become solid, touching rooftops and trees. If it does not rain, if the clouds move and sun breaks through, I will take her to the park this afternoon, to play on the grass.

4

The curtains are drawn back. It is high summer now, the longest day of the year. I have watched the light change from grey to gold, fade from bluish grey to grow pale, white, and now the whole sky is flushed with streaks of pink and gold. Soon the sun will rise, but already the day is alive, the trees at the bottom of the garden are singing, thousands of birds are singing from behind a thousand leaves, as though knowing the sun will rise, as though willing it upward in a chorus. I did not know such a multitude of small voices could be at one and the same time, nor that so many birds lived concealed in the city. It has become a huge garden, no sound from streets still sunk in bluish shadow, light touches the rising walls of houses, gold gleams on the edges of glass, touches dark, crumbling old brickwork which stands like rocks in this garden alive with so much colour and sound. And behind those shadowy curtained windows now touched with first light, inside those brick bastions bodies lie unaware, eyes closed, deaf. Sleeping as always, year in and out. Until now I have heard nothing, seen nothing. I slept like somebody drugged by habit.

But now I am awake, as though for the first time. My body is a landscape which I have been exploring, through the night I have found small unexpected hollows, hidden valleys, cool wind now thrilling glacier slopes, soft curving downs and the newfound ridge which is my spine. A lava of salt sweat has cooled between my breasts, flaccid hills with volcanic tips, and trickled down to the small round tarn of my navel. Odours of marsh and bog come from it when I move slightly, I shift the hard rock of my pelvis and feel how it runs, sticky, through the bushy thicket from the pothole, the dark passage of rock with its cave beyond. I am tired, having slept only fitfully, worn out with the effort of running, climbing, panting for breath up the final rockface, clinging on, clutching his hair, undergrowth, narrow ledges of bone on the hard shoulder, till I got up there, in the dark, to drop off, falling into the dark, and find myself, still lying in my own landscape, in dim light with the sky fading.

I heard the dawn chorus begin, until a thousand birds sang into a fading sky. I lie, and a thousand birds are singing, under my skin, in tingling nerve ends. The pores of my skin feel the moving air, taking it in, breathing, small hairs rise and curve like reeds in a shivering stream.

I am alive, at last I am fully alive. I feel as though I had only just begun, though my life is half over, counting in years, what is absurdly called the best part. Now it is high summer, and if it has come late, it has come. I have not waited to no purpose, or kept faith for nothing. This morning is a new dawn, which has the sound and colour of pure joy. I lie, hearing how the birds sing, how the branches of trees are stirred and burst into leaf and song long before sunrise, while the sky is still clear but nacreous. I have hardly slept, but through my fatigue I am fully alive. It is as though I had travelled an immense distance and now, finding myself lying back in my old room, the furniture is familiar but disturbed, curious. I see the heaviness of the old oak chest, the dark marks ingrained in the wood. The long oval mirror in the corner of the room shines with reflections of night fading. A chair has been moved, and stands at an odd angle. His clothes lie, showing linings and seams. The air smells of skin, tobacco and sex.

His head on the pillow looks large. This bed is narrow for two, and I lie on my side watching the curve of his mouth, short dark hairs on his forearm round my shoulder, the flat brown nipple near my mouth. I breathe in the smell of his skin. He lies flat on his back, leaving me almost no room in the narrow bed. My neck is in the crook of his elbow, his left leg between both of mine. My shoulder aches but I do not shift, for fear of disturbing him. Instead I lift my arm and lightly touch the black curled hair close to his ear. It springs back into position under my touch. I notice a tremor under his eyelids, he moves his head from side to side on the pillow and his lips move as though he is about to say something. Now the head is still. My mouth touches the part of his body close by, skin which is remarkably soft and white. His lips curve in a smile. Now his whole body shifts, under his weight the mattress heaves and I am enclosed by him, his odour, the shadow of his body cuts off light. A numb limb now tingles as blood begins to flow, his hair tickles my face, bristle rubs my raw mouth, his breath is warm, warm air comes from the fetid hollows of his body and I breathe them in, gladly. He runs his hand down the cool skin of my back and shoulder blade. His fingers find the jutting bones of my spine and press down, feeling each hard nub in turn, like keys of an instrument. I am trapped, enclosed by his sleeping body which enfolds me. I can feel his heart beat, his warm breath sounds in my ear. I feel newborn: folded petals of flesh lying inside harsh brown leaves. I lie very still, listening to his sleeping breath, a slight grunt or hitch in his throat. Beyond the curve of his heavy shoulder I see light from the window.

I hear sounds from the garden, but nothing from beyond the wall. It is early, they sleep as though drugged through dovegrey light turning to mother-of-pearl, through the dawn chorus shrilling from the full green leaf of plane and chestnut tree. But I hear and see all things, like somebody newborn. I have left behind those dark winter days, sitting alone in a darkening room, hearing my own footfalls echo in empty streets after nightfall, turning away, saying no, hearing the false courage of my voice as, my hand on the light switch, I told my children to go to sleep, nothing to fear, sitting in a room ringed with deepening shadows, lamplight falling on the book open in my lap. I would stand at the window watching windows across the dark street, somebody walk across a room as though on stage, in a lit box.

50

Having walked through the door the frame went black. Later, lying awake in the small hours, I heard thunder roll over the rooftops. Within seconds one small body, then two, had crawled shivering under the bedclothes and dug into my sides. Comforted, they slept soundly within moments. Hemmed in, feeling their warmth, I dozed uneasily till morning.

I must put a lock on my door. We cannot always be saying shush, holding our breath, stopping, each time we think we hear something that could be a thump, thud, or words cried out from a dream, fearful, thinking is he awake, is she coming now? It is risky, the unexpected, and for them the night is full of terrors: the moon a presence, evil, leering into the room from the sky, wild animals lurk in cupboards, nightmares surfacing into fright until they come running across the dark landing to find me, my body, its warmth. If they should find a naked man lurking in the dark . . .

I smile now, lying in my soft new skin. Knowing how unfailingly he could win them: a trip to the zoo, mending a mechanical toy would be enough. Perhaps a picnic in woods, walk over hills and drive back. Things which bind us, the simplicity of doing. So much, so easy, to do. How easy it is to be happy, now.

My body is awake after its long winter. It sings, it blossoms. I know it from head to foot, supple, as supple as a young girl now. It has come at last, the summer of my life. I have walked through brightly lit rooms in which people talked, laughed, and come away, closing the door behind me, walked down dark streets leaving those lights and voices behind me, into a darkness which was solitary.

51

A steady ache in my ribcage recurred. Nobody in the room had remotely resembled him, I had looked at each face in turn until words ceased to have meaning, they fell round me like coins clattering onto a stone floor, eyes had a glazed look as though the owner had gone home an hour ago, nobody lived behind them, the whole room was a charade, a phantasmagoria of wild sounds, thick smoke and ugly music. And I was one of them. Did the others have a similar pain under their ribs, did the glazed look in the eyes come from a sense of unreality? Did they listen to their own voices with incredulity, the words flowing of their own accord, a reflex laugh coming in spasm, oh how it hurt, knowing I do not know you, your eyes are glazed and do not even see me, perhaps because I am not here?

Winter was dark and hollow. I was hollow, perhaps it was that which gave me a constant pain. I was brave for the sake of the children, smiled when they whimpered at nightfall, told happy stories till they slept, of childhood lived through woods and meadows and a stream which ran through a constant summer, I stroked their heads and spoke soothing words when they crawled shivering under my bedclothes in the small hours of the night, pressed close to my body, having seen a ghost, the face of the moon peering in, or a bad dream. But, in the dark, my uncurtained windows were huge wounds exposed to the cold night. Anybody could have looked in and seen how it was, how I stood staring out, a solitary figure, with the lamp lit behind me, and nobody in the room. Stood for hours, it seemed, staring down at the road, the houses opposite, my elbows pressed on the window sill. Or walked from room to room, each one empty, waiting, and the telephone silent in the hall.

Now it is past and finished. Summer has come, my life is now at its zenith. From now on I will live it to the full, the few good years that still lie ahead. In spite of everything, I was right to hold on through dark nights and grey mornings, endure, refuse to settle for less, hold on to the truth which I felt must exist even though I had no proof, only my own instinct, though time was passing and I knew that my own days were finite, soon I would grow old, die, so what was I waiting for? But I did wait, and now I am glad, in spite of the wasted days, no, because of them, since crawling through an underground tunnel is black on account of the light and colour above ground, since the hollow pain which ached in my ribcage signified a missing element, which by its nature, being missing, could be found.

The light grows more intense beyond the curve of his shoulder. His arm pulls in tight round my body, his mouth finds my face. Still, luckily, I hear no sound of children waking through the wall between my room and theirs. Odd how human beings can sleep so soundly through such a shrill chorus of birds, light turning the window frame to gold, glinting obliquely on glass, buried in the long mirror. I smile into the colour and sound of summer breaking overhead, still growing.

He has opened his eyes. For a moment it is as though he has never opened them before. I look at him, and he smiles back. His face lies close to mine on the pillow, now he draws back slightly, as though to look at me whole. Dark black rings round his irises fade as he wakes. My mouth is dry: it tastes of him. He runs the tip of his finger down the length of my nose and across half my mouth. I trap the tip between my teeth, and with my mouth closed begin to suck. I can sense how he feels the texture of my tongue. I let go and he puts his mouth in the hollow of my neck which has a knot of newfound nerve ends, sending feeling down the length of my body. His hands now mould it, breast and pelvis, the curve of my neck, the sharp angle of my clavicle and the vertebrae running down the back of my neck and between my shoulder blades. He holds my head, it becomes a round object, he lifts it between his hands like a drinking vessel, my skull is a gourd, I feel full of some sweet fluid, how the sap rises from my trunk to flow into his mouth, while his mouth is on mine, his hands clutch and tip my head, some precious trickle runs up the inside fur of my belly as his tongue licks the walls of the cave which is my mouth. Our tongues touch, feel each other, two subterranean slugs with rough and slimy skins, fat and round, animals capable of exploring the sharp contours of bone, soft walls of flesh in the dark. How absurd, such antediluvian antics, polymorphic sea slugs in their black caves, sharp rows of stalactites, those are my teeth, the sea slug darts back and forth through its row of defensive rocks, but how much it tells me, how quick and how deep it penetrates. The skin round my mouth is sore. Breathless, we let go our hold and lie.

Cold air runs down one side of my body. His weight presses on the other half of it. He props himself up on his elbow to watch my face, but when I open my eyes I see a tangle of my own hair, luminous at the edges. I pull back a strand caught in the corner of my mouth. The sweat between our skins begins to cool. It will run down to my navel, which is deep and round as a pool. I think of a tarn seen on top of a bare hillside. His navel is different. I think about accidental things, like birth. How somebody gave birth to him, in a different place. I pity his mother and mine, for being dead, or old, for having done it so long ago, before we were born.

But I have time left, though not too much. The good days are finite now, I can almost count them, like a short string of beads. The summer will fade to the chill mists of autumn, after which come the dark nights, snow and death. I will notice the first signs, leaves turning colour, lengthening shadows on the lawn in the late afternoon, the long goodbye glowing fiercely in the stretching hold of trees. The summer will fade in the light of a distant sun, perhaps the last summer. But now, from my window, I see how the sky is flushed with an early sunrise of pink and gold. A perfect day lies ahead. Through the wall I hear how a child sighs, turns, murmurs something from its dream, and lies sunk and still.

Light touches the walls of this room, gleams in the long oval mirror. In the night I trod barefoot across the floor, stepping over the handwoven carpet, wool dyed the colour of clotted blood, and saw how I gleamed out of the dark behind me, caught in the falling lamplight I saw a heavy-breasted, forked creature caught in the shadows of the long oval mirror. I moved closer and stood, shocked, staring into the wild eyes, black, burning, which looked out from skin not just glowing, but incandescent, a white shape with a head surrounded by a wild bush of confused hair. So this is me, I thought. I have become a burning torch.

The lamp still burns feebly against the wall, a yellow discarded husk. Clarity touches all things, pores, textures, a crack in the wall beside the wardrobe, brown shadows under his closed lids, short dark lashes, blue veins marbled under white skin. My mouth is dry. In the quiet room I hear my gut rumble and squelch loudly before becoming still. My arm is numb from his weight. I think about withdrawing it, of disturbing him. His foot touches my foot. I move my toes. Now his curved instep runs up the hard smooth incline of my left shin.

I am inside my body, heavy, but also light. It has taken a long time to come to this. I think about the day ahead, which will be unlike those I have known. I am divided by a curtain of light from those days, when I counted the time of my life which had already gone, feeling my ribs tight as I stood under an empty sky, saying: soon I will be old. How I stood in an empty room, hearing the sound of traffic from the dark road, in a hurry, stood with the ring of lamplight falling on the rug and my own shoes and heard a voice in my head say now, my body is here now, the petals will fall after this, my body is ready now, as only something living and growing rises and then falls from its zenith.

The light is blocked out by the mass of his head above mine. His mouth finds mine, it is greedy now, the weight of his body presses down with a gravity it did not have before, I hear how the bedsprings squeak, louder, the sound is embarrassing now, I find myself trying to hear beyond, through the wall in case the children are listening, his mouth tastes of stale tobacco and semen, beyond his head I see the outline of an empty wineglass, its clearness smudged, reddish brown dregs where the stem begins, saliva cools on my face which is raw with his stubble. I must conceal the traces with powder. I must make breakfast soon. I am willing to appease him, his hungry body, but my own is cold, distant. I do not mind. Night will come back. Gratification is hit and miss, now my body is worn out, used. I will stagger through the day like a drunk with lack of sleep. Perhaps an early night would be a good idea. I stroke his shoulders. I press down my right foot to contain a seizure of cramp. I lick his ear in a frenzy, moan, clutch his body tight to make him come, come now, finish at long last. I stroke his head after the final seizure, twisting his hair between my fingers, as though he was a small boy, my child. I smile at the ceiling. Gratification, gratitude, sweat cooling on the surface of our bodies. He murmurs words I want to hear, he kisses and touches lightly now, the curve of one breast, my throat. I raise one arm and look at it. He looks at it also and lifts his arm to meet it, palms touching, fingers interlaced. He brings down his arm to look at his wristwatch.

'I must go,' he says.

5

Grey light. Put myself together. Pull myself together. No. Who am I? Oh yes, I have a name. I move in the old bed and begin to feel how my leg joins to the pelvis. Somewhere under the covers lie the remnants of a body, with little or no life. Except that it aches. And I have nausea. The body is sluggish, the skin tingles, now blood is running down my other leg, painfully. I still have both feet, I know, since I was able to move both just now. But the pain in my side is back. Oh no.

Oh yes. I have a name, a place in time. Must I remember? I am afraid so. It is coming back, if slowly. Life is a river which becomes sluggish as it reaches the endless sea. I have found a hand, though as yet it does not seem to be attached. I dreamt that I was a young girl, but this is untrue. For the past few nights I have found myself pleading for my future, quivering on the brink, one might say, and always young. I know what my unconscious is trying to tell me, but it is deceitful. Just now I stood in the law court, waited to be heard in a long stone corridor. Grey light from tall windows. The man in the black robe who heard my petition was the lawyer who dealt with my divorce petition. I could not see his face. It could have been the master who taught me pain and servitude at school, that building also had long stone corridors and grey light coming through tall windows. How absurd. He stood with his face hidden by deep shadows and would not speak. He listened though, I am almost certain of that.

The torso under the bedclothes belongs to me, no doubt about that now. I wish it were not so, since the ache in my side is so familiar. Slowly I find the connecting links between my head and other bits, reluctant to admit the inescapable. This place in time is not what I would wish for. I have a name, a place in time, but I am no longer myself. Perhaps I am the young girl, trying to escape in dreams during the night, a body which has ceased to conform to anything I recognize as me. I think of an old doll, its members dislocated: each morning it is painfully re-assembled. I think how the river runs downhill and becomes sluggish in the final estuary. Such images belong to my childhood.

I think of the day ahead and see only cold grey light. I find it impossible to conceive that I could ever, should ever find the will necessary to rise and become vertical.

Grey light. Winter. Yet another February morning, hard as iron, relentless, a cold light which could come from a steel sky. I have no wish to continue the charade which is my life, not now, not while I lie with the familiar small ache in my side and nausea taking the place of a normal appetite. I presume I used to wake up hungry, though I cannot remember. Once I am upright it will begin to take hold, first I will move stiffly, like a clock-work mechanism, until gradually, as the day moves forward I become the person who is doing all those things which are expected or perhaps even necessary. But not now. Eventually, I know, getting up becomes more of a necessity than lying down, if only because I have to go to the bathroom.

Nothing is quite as it should be. I wake back into a world in which everything has become uncontrollable, is going wrong in unforeseen ways. My body, for instance, it has suddenly become a dead weight, something with which I am at odds. I drag it around and see everything through its slightly jaundiced eyes. And for months now, or is it years, this house has been at odds with itself, doors close violently, voices rise in rage, the family has grown into an invading force from which I would like to try and escape, or at least hide. Why else should I have such dreams, in which I plead to be recognized as a young girl, recurring night after night, as though clamouring on a locked door? Drifts of mist hang over my waking thoughts, uneasy traces of a disturbed mind. I rise each morning with a layer of detritus, dead matter, old skin clinging to me, an invisible web of dust, cobwebs, falling hair and the skeletal outline of dried leaves which I cannot shake off. Something terrible has begun, that is why I feel so bad first thing in the morning. Inside something must have given way, walls have begun to leak or crumble, so I do not function as I should. I think about the organs which lie under the skin, according to the diagrams in textbooks, which I have not had to think about before now. Perhaps it is my liver which aches. I am vague about the functions of the liver, and even of its exact position. But I feel bad. I do not feel myself. I do not wish to get up and confront the hollow, even slightly horrific face which will look back at me from the glass. Self-hatred. She looks at me with loathing and disgust, the sick face which resembles my mother. No, I wish to say, it is not true, looking back at the slack grey folds of skin which seem to be sucked inward between cheekbone and jaw, but nothing will belie the fact. Even those eyes are not mine. Flat, lacking in depth, dull and tired, the eyes of a woman who has given up the ghost, but who is ashamed of defeat.

A cold winter morning, relentless, the light hard as iron, a cutting edge of steel. Just two short months from now and spring will have begun, the dark days of winter lived through and packed away. Hope. Melting and soft, inconceivable now, at this moment. Sunlight and warm air. The possibility of love. A dusting of pale green, like powder, outside each window where now a network of twigs and branches shows black on white, traced with a sharp pen. My body moving freely in loose clothes, and warm air blowing through an open window, lifting curtains and loose papers which fly from the table onto the floor. A warm gust which brings in a scent of grass, and birds singing.

Each year I live in hope, that things will change when spring comes. And occasionally it has been so, something has occurred, and for a few days of high summer my life has been transformed, just as long as it took the heavy chestnut blossom to drop in thick drifts on the shaded pavement, for the roses to burst and blow away, for the first leaves of autumn to shrivel and drop. The sun shone, and I was happy. But now summers, when they do occur, have become too short, not long enough for me to thaw out after such long winters, dark unbroken days which have imposed themselves on my spirit, cold seeps through the old brick walls of this house and settles in my bones. The cold has got to me, muscles ache with it, joints stiff and brittle with frost, the face in the mirror is frostbitten, pinched with winter. Always I am conscious of the dark beyond the circle of lamplight, closing me in, trapping me, how big the night beyond, until now I hardly move without being conscious of its numbing power. I recall my childhood, waking to sunlight, a time when the sun always shone, a day of unending summer days. How the cock crew, and the curtain blew into the room. But now the arc of winter has grown, till summer has become only a brief interlude, so short I can count the days. And now I think: only two more months. When spring comes, will it bring any improvement? And I am conscious that not only days but also my years are running short, that each life has only so many chances when the light returns. The likelihood is, I am too old for a rebirth.

I listen for sounds in the next room, but so far nobody is awake. They sleep so soundly. I did too, at that age, round the clock sometimes, to wake fresh as a daisy. Not now. Everything grubby, surfaces cracking. The house is subsiding, it creaks in the night as I turn, feeling the ache in my right side, in a high wind at midnight

I hear a loose wood strip rattle in the hollow spaces under the roof, last year, or was it the winter before, pigeons broke in under the gutter and woke me during the night with their frantic nest-building. Once, during the summer, we heard mice scampering noisily under the floorboards; no sign during the day except tiny black droppings, but in the nights they nibbled their way through the larder. I had to throw out spoiled packages and put down poison. But this last invasion is the worst. I am not at ease in my own house. I wait for the first sounds, tense, listening. I wish this time, of listening, waiting for it to be finished with, was finished with now. It is anyhow a period of slow death, a kind of killing, this second parturition.

So far nobody has stirred, but soon I will hear their voices and the rhythmic squeak of the bedsprings. I am supposed to be jealous, because of my age. No, decidedly not. I would laugh, if I did not pity them. But my instinct is at odds with principles. I do not wish to know, or hear: I do not want to be disturbed in my own house.

I lie tense in my own room now because they have turned me into an intruder, in my own house. If I now get up I could encounter one of them on the landing, going into or coming from the bathroom and be made to feel culpable for not turning invisible in my own house, this old woman, they say, and somebody else's child who has stayed all night without my permission will slip by with averted eyes, as the next best thing. I should, their lowered heads tell me, not be here. But my own child, his mouth soft as rubber under the ugly stubble he refuses to remove, his head set rigid as he looks down at me from his newfound height, will go further: you are ugly, he tells me, you are hideous and old. And if his mouth holds back the words his eyes challenge me. Why don't you go away, he asks, and drop into a hole in the ground? Cover yourself up, he says, walking through my door without knocking, your body is disgusting. And once, in a mood of false jollity he cracked what he maintained was a joke: Why don't you jump out of the window, so I could have this place to myself? Under the circumstances I was not amused, and said so. It was only a joke, he retorted sulkily. As though he kept no guard on his subconscious. But of course he does. He walks through the rooms of his childhood holding himself rigid in what amounts to an uncomfortable suit of armour, makes loud clattering noises, spars furiously with battered furniture and swinging doors, glares at any man who dares to cross the threshold through his visor, holding his face rigid, and refuses to allow me to be anything but the horrid old hag who must be turned into a mere wisp of smoke or a pile of dead rags. I try to hold my own, but he knows when my spirit is low and presses the point home. Soon I will get up and confirm what he sees in the long glass. Yesterday he told me, knowing how it would hurt, you are beginning to look like Granny, and as he spoke I felt how my thin lips closed grimly over patched teeth and shrinking gums. Not enough flesh, I thought, sensing her expression grow tight under my skin, and hating it.

I do not want to get up. I do not want to see myself in the long mirror. And it is cold. I lie tensed against the cold, huddled inside the bedclothes. Should I see a doctor about the pain in my side? Yes. No. Probably inconclusive, how it is with vague chronic symptoms. Tedious and boring, sitting in out-patient departments, wasting an afternoon or a whole day getting in and out of clothes in cubicles, waiting to be X-rayed. To be told something I do not want to hear. Anyhow, they know nothing until it becomes obvious to a simpleton. But this is no way to live. I force myself to eat, fighting down nausea, assuming it is better to eat. Every morning.

How long can I keep going, through the motions, forcing myself up on each bleak winter morning, simply because there are things to do? But I must. I must buy food, go to the bank, go to the hospital this afternoon. I live on the edge of chaos, inside and out, I live from day to day with the walls crumbling in, trying to hold it back just one more hour, stop the masonry from burying part of me. But I know it is only a matter of time, I am holding out by the hour, I know that chaos has come for good. So I will go to the hospital once more, disrupting my schedule, no, it has become part of it, my regular day, but always it is a rush, a panic, will she look bad, should I buy flowers this time or something she could perhaps swallow, I try hard to shed the panic on the hospital staircase, that is why I climb to the second floor instead of using the lift, when I look through the glass of her cubicle I smile, trying to look calm, trying to put out of my head my own anxious thoughts, my own troubles which I am used to sharing with her, even now she wants me to tell her, but I think how selfish, when she is suffering, knowing it must end, she must leave it all behind, the troubles we divided between us, difficult sons, rebellious or sulky daughters and our own fury, she knows I

66

must carry on without her, so she is kind and very calm in the white cubicle, between spasms of pain, I hold her thin hand with the loose heavy rings, or perhaps she is holding mine, I do not know, and neither of us knows who is in most need of comfort, she who must go or I who must continue with nobody to comfort me, hold my hand or listen to my troubles, which will continue. Since she knows this is the end she has become quite calm, open, her face has a washed look, like the face of a child, it is soothed with relief which makes it easy for us, when only a few weeks ago she clung so desperately to the idea of living, buying things she would never use, clothes she could not wear while she talked of going to Paris, perhaps Rome, though even as she whispered a few words her strength was used up, all she wanted to do was lean back against the high pillows and close her eyes while I dimmed the lights and walked on tiptoe towards the door. My time was up.

I must get up. So much to do. It cannot go on much longer, this dreadful time, and then it will be worse. I try not to think of it, so selfish. I must think only of her. But a small voice is crying in my head: what am I to do, when it is over, and I have nobody?

Yesterday she wanted to know about my daughter, had things improved? I shook my head. It takes time, she whispered. I am ashamed of my life, how messy it is, and so futile and petty. I do not want to speak of it, but it seems she still wants to hear. I am doubly ashamed because when her daughter left home I could not condone the fury which shook her, I was critical and unsympathetic, having not so far reached that stretch of the road. I am following behind her, just a few years. She looks back at the road along which I struggle with a detached, almost ethereal calm, in spite of the odour of death, her face pale, eyes glowing with warmth, perhaps pity, in those few moments which are free of pain. How many years before I lie in her place?

I want to push it all into the background, the accumulation of failure, loss, nothing has turned out as I intended it should, when I was so sure I knew how, and why, and now the structures are falling down anyhow, the pain in my side, nobody to turn to, the world full of dying. That happy band which was us is now a group of ghosts, dead or still living, but carrying the imprint of those others, the grey cobwebs of death in our faces, caught in our hair. I move into a world of silence, and it fills me with terror. The telephone will not ring. I will not speak to anybody. I will walk through a landscape of tombstones under a darkening sky.

I never thought it would be like this. That in spite of everything I could do, thinking, reading, preparing the mind, each event should find me totally unprepared, like a thunderbolt coming suddenly from between normal grey clouds. So, having told myself for years, his health is not good, you must be prepared, and he also took care to warn us, nevertheless when the telephone call came in the middle of the night I panicked, could not find my clothes, as I drove along empty roads through the dark I felt sick, my hands shook and I was quite unprepared for what I was to find, thinking of a false alarm, the message anyhow garbled, perhaps to spare us, something about a disturbed night, but when I was told unequivocally, your father is going to die, I was angry, refused to accept, such a harsh prognosis, how dare he, I thought, his job is to save life, only a charge nurse anyhow, and demanded to see the doctor. And when the young doctor arrived and told us the same thing we spent a futile morning making telephone calls, to the family doctor, discussed specialists, anybody who would contradict, until we had to give up trying and turn into the cruel morning of bright sunshine. And we stood, such a fine morning of high summer, roses in the hospital flower-beds, watching the sun climb up, up into a clear roseate sky, unable to do anything but hold on, to our shaking bodies, wishing the sun would stop rising. And afterwards I was numb, as though the event had nothing to do with ordinary things, not until the funeral, when I saw the box with my father inside, I knew he was inside and the shock made me cry. I stopped being numb. It was good, it broke through the fog. But since then my head has been full of unfinished business, it occurs to me at odd hours, how we tried so hard to pretend that nothing serious was going on, as though to spare each other, but it was wrong, now we are left in a limbo of unspoken words and small wrong turnings.

But it is not hard to go to her, not now. Not since she knows, and accepts. For so long we have been doing this gruesome double act on the high wire, with courage, assuredly, with grim jokes and wry humour, I have come to her bedside armed with spiky flowers, sharp jokes and a bundle of bitchy gossip to make us laugh, and watched her mimic the sad painted clown. But now there is no need to continue, we have stepped down from the high wire, and touched solid ground. It is a relief. For her. But I must continue without her, waking up each morning to this unease, this household where we have outgrown each other so that nobody belongs. It is hard to live as a survivor.

So now I lie awake in self-hatred, not wishing to accept what I have become, feeling the tense line of my mouth, how the gums have shrunk, my cheeks loose and sallow, so that I know how I look, sour-faced and tired. I do not want to get up and look at myself in the long mirror, even if I could ignore the ache in my side and nausea rising, nothing will bring back the person I used to be, who smiled at herself in the glass, acknowledging the pleasure of a curve, the depth of those dark eyes, lustrous, shining in a double complicity, as they smiled back. What happened to her? I do not know, only that she slipped away one night, is now dead, will not come back, that I am doomed to drag about this other body who fills me with disgust, whom I do not like, nobody could. Eyes in the street, standing on platforms, sitting opposite in the underground slide away, glance past or look straight through me as though I did not exist, that was when I first knew something had happened, that the person I had always been was dead, that nothing I did or could do would bring her back.

I must get up, soon. I ought to see a doctor. Something is definitely wrong. I doubt, though, whether he can do much. Something is crumbling, breaking down inside, the changes are too subtle, somehow too final, for human intervention. My mouth tastes sour, my breath putrid: I know the signs. I have winced with disgust when my father kissed me, trying not to smell his bad breath. Now the odour is on me, I know it, and my children have less discretion in voicing their disgust. Probably he knew, though, as I turned my mouth away and offered him the side of my cheek. His memory must have told him.

This afternoon I will go to the hospital and smell the odour of her dying wound. It surrounds her. It is always in my nostrils now, however hard I try to deny it. It is the smell of death, of all our yesterdays falling behind, rotting like old leaves. Children are very cruel. They do not know what it is, the division between body and spirit, when the mind disowns the body in which it is trapped. For two years now they have passed on the other side of the closed door as though nothing was happening, tried to ignore it, the odour of the sick room not stifled by flowers, time measured by pills and recurring pain in constant artificial light. It is too close to concealed resentment, stifled wishes, not just disgust but the wish to break free, to be acknowledged. Mine would, in fact do, the same in a different way. We stand in the doorway, block out the light, through which they need to pass.

Looking back, how good it was, only a few short years ago. We did not know how good life was. We took the children on outings to the park, the woods on the heath, we always wanted to lose them for a bit, closed the playroom door, longing for quiet and adult conversation, sat in a haze of smoke and discussed whether a good life was possible, by which we meant love, relationships with men. She wanted marriage, something stable, more dependable than anything either of us had known. And I? Could I have got more than tension, excitement, what

I had, given the need always to look for more, something beyond the horizon? What fun it was, those dark hours of Saturday in winter when we sat through rather silly films to keep the kids amused, hours we thought could have been better spent if it had not been for them, buying packets of popcorn, toffee papers stuck to our clothes, driving back to a scratch supper before it was time to take them home to bed. They played games, laughed, shrieked and quarrelled in the other room while we sat in the kitchen drinking coffee. Go away, she said: leave us in peace. And shook ash from her clothes into the brimming ashtray. You smoke too much I said, lightly, knowing it would do no good, and she shrugged: there has to be *some* pleasure in life.

And then suddenly it was over. They did go away, to come back at odd hours. They did not come running, demanding to be in the centre of our eyes, holding on to our laps, mouths, hands. Now they tried to slink past unheard from the front door to the staircase, unwilling to be confronted, constantly in a group in which they hid, seeking protection, whispering, smuggling contraband and glancing across a ring of shoulders towards the outside world. We outside in that world. Confronting them, they would explode in a sudden rage, hostile, cold, suddenly all the familiar rituals had begun to disintegrate and we broke gifts, tore down holly and mistletoe, then sat alone in the empty room in a haze of smoke drinking whisky, taking comfort from the fact that we had both behaved badly, irrationally, without understanding the rage which fractured us.

Time to go through the motion of living. Now I hear

sounds through the wall: a dull thud, he murmurs something, her voice in a different octave answers back, high and clear. I feel excluded, an intruder in my own house. Perhaps it is time to die, to shrivel up unnoticed in a dusty corner. That is what his eyes say. No, you must assert yourself, forget how tired you have become. Get up, put the kettle on, make breakfast. Some day in the near future there will be a fight, and you will have to push this fledgling out of the nest, before he tramples you to death. Ugly, I do not like it, but no doubt it is a necessary part of the cycle. I am a tool of evolution, though it feels wrong.

Put some clothes on, quickly. Anything to avoid this chill, it bites through like death. Thick, anonymous, pull something under. Do not stand naked in the room. Avoid his eye on the landing. Wool, the colour of dun, something old and shabby, shapeless and worn. Outside I have become invisible in the dull stone light of winter, until I suddenly catch a glimpse, in some mottled patch of coated glass, a shadow moving across shopfronts, of a woman wrapped up against the cold. Her eyes light up, hurt and twisted, seeing them peer helplessly through two holes of pinched wintry flesh in the vivid patch of mottled mirror. I walk on quickly to the underground station.

6

So. I am back in this old room. It hangs loose, like old skin. Grey light falls on a film of grey dust. The light is of grey dust, it has settled on the furniture, seeped into the walls. I can feel it tickle my nostrils as I breathe in. This dusty grey dawn settles on my skin each morning. I cannot shake it out of my hair. I open my eyes to a faded photograph of a curtained window, light falling under its folds, seeping between dusty faded edge and window frame, falling onto the worn carpet with its faded colours which once glowed in summer light, amber and the colour of dried blood. I do not know how many times I have opened my eyes into this room, the film of grey images fall, one on another, superimpose, and now I look at an old familiar photograph.

I have a book of photographs in my head. This is only one of them. Perhaps I am only looking at the room from outside, turning the pages of my album. I do this often nowadays. Sometimes I think, when I die I will not notice much difference, or perhaps this is already a sort of death, a kind of preparation, since my mind is detached from the act of waking, each grey dawn is a kind of limbo while my mind takes in the fact that light is indeed coming from the window, filtering round the edges of the hung cloth at top and bottom of the heavy window frame and also down the centre, where my hands have drawn the two curtains together. Close, but not quite close enough. Each morning I find a gap through which the light falls, onto the dusty surface of the table, and below it to the carpet patterned with dying amber and drops of dry blood.

Each morning is so much like yesterday morning that my mind is numb for a bit. First I think, I am looking at a familiar photograph, or rather, a faded offprint which becomes a little dimmer, a little more indistinct each time I open my eyes. Afterwards, and sometimes this happens quickly, on first opening my eyes, I know that I am neither dreaming nor regarding a photograph, but that I am a person who has quite simply woken up. This gives me an unpleasant ache under my ribs which may continue for some minutes, and is not unlike heartache felt in the old days. But now I feel it at no other time, and mostly the discomfort is over within seconds.

In a sense I am born each morning. That is what I feel, and find terrible for a brief moment, until I become accustomed to this old room and cold light falling from the window. The familiarity of this room, in which each piece of heavy furniture has stood for so long where it now stands, intruding into the room, occupying dusty space, is a reality I find unacceptable. So much so that I go away for weeks at a time for no reason except to avoid the mingling of our dust and the feeling that I am born each morning into the same four walls where each thing stands as it has stood without my once having counted the days, while we grow grey together, gathering dust, cracks in the ceiling, a hair of grey cobweb floating in shadows. As though that is not bad enough, being born into such a familiar space, my movements would be measured out like those of an automaton by the width between bed and wardrobe, the number of paces possible from window to door, long mirror to chair to old oak chest. So I pack a suitcase and go for the pleasure of coming back, so that I may feel a visitor in my own room when I unpack and get into bed.

Because that is what I am, nowadays, a ghost in a faded photograph. I am surrounded by silence. By a void which it is my duty to fill. I am a visitor in my own room, uncommitted, using superfluous time. But I have to be reminded occasionally, the human mind being a victim of habit. Then I go away for a bit, leave this room to come back. So that I may hear the silence. It frightens me occasionally, but on good days it is an element which holds all things in unity. I now find it preferable to the human voice, and even music is only a variation of it. No sound comes through the wall, now that the house is empty. But through the silence I hear all things.

I inhabit each day as it comes, slowly, once the pain of waking has subsided. Because waking is a shock, and it takes a little while to accept the fact that I am still alive, still here, for the faded photograph to become solid, for the pain of the light coming through the window heavy with unused hours to lift.

After the solidity of light and windowframe have been established I must also revive my body, since only my head wakes. This is a slow business nowadays, but I am in no hurry. I am reminded of a fumbling hand trying to inhabit an old leather glove. The glove is familiar, well worn, so much so that it never loses the singular contours of this hand, but overnight, each night, it has been dropped and forgotten on the midnight lawns of sleep which are white with hoar frost. By dawn it is stiff and hard from exposure, and I cannot enter it. It hurts to try. I feel how my mind moves downward, cautiously, trying to avoid sudden discomfort. Stiff, numb, I turn slowly, hoping to subdue sudden anguish as blood begins to tingle down the side on which I was lying. I move an arm, my head, and feel how certain joints ache as I do so. But it seems as though I will be able to move out of the bed.

One more day. I come back slowly, letting go of the child in my arms, how he wriggled to escape my clutches, as a child will do, slithering with his soft buttocks in my palms before I woke and remembered he is a man now, with a child of his own. Nowadays my sleep is all flesh, turgid with sex, I toss and turn in his shadow, it is on me, round me, I surround it, the dark shadow of a man who makes me grasp, twitch in spasm. Without a face, and quite without emotion. My body is a landscape, a bubbling quagmire across which the shadow falls.

During the day I do not think of such things. Not

78

because it would be ridiculous, unseemly, to expose my sagging flesh to scrutiny under lamplight, drop my clothes on the patterned carpet glowing amber and blood as I once did in the old days, though it would be an undoubted embarrassment. But because I am calm now, free of such notions. I cannot remember the last time I looked at a man and said yes, you. I regard love as a virus, an idiotic feverish condition which I have survived to become immune, and sane. Though it did, of course, give colour to colourless days.

Another grey day coming through the window.

Of course, it will not remain grey. I have learnt to colour them in, like a child with a colouring book. That is the secret. But to begin with, all the pages are blank, a uniform cloud colour. It is the shade I notice on first waking, though I am not sure whether it comes from in my head, or if the hangings and the quality of light itself can have faded so much. What shall I do, a child's voice cries, distant and small. Colour it in, the teacher's voice replies. The world is full of small unnoticed things which need to be noticed. Small things in their turn make up perfection.

My head is full of them now. I collect them during the day. Since I have begun to do this the hours are almost too short for my purpose. By the time I go back to bed the pages are full of impressions. And so much I will not be able to record, not now. I am filled with gratitude for such plenitude. As a child I collected grains of sand for their shape and colour and felt a similar emotion at such an infinity all round me, from which I could choose, which nobody saw, only I saw the particles of ruby, emerald and crystal. The adult world walked down the path: it was only sand.

It began with the silence. I woke in the morning and no sound came through the wall. The room was empty. All the rooms were unoccupied. For the first time there was nobody to listen for, tense, anxious or hopeful. There was, in the terms I understood from a lifetime of waking, nothing to wake up for. No reason to get up. All my life I had woken up and begun the day because of some imposed necessity. When I was a child I longed to be up first, but I had to wait until my mother came into the room. I was thrust out of sullen sleep on dark mornings so as not to be late for school, or work. An alarm clock jangled, somebody shook my shoulder. A child woke screaming with appendicitis in the small hours. It was necessary that they should not be late for school. Occasionally I woke early and lay contemplating the day ahead. Until sounds came through the wall and it had begun.

Now I woke into silence, and at first it was a terrifying experience. To lie alone in an empty house with a choice, clear and unmistakable, do I get up or not, knowing that it makes no difference, nobody will be angry, anxious, nobody is getting hungry, watching the clock, nobody will mind. It is entirely up to you, whether you get up.

Why did I get up, that first morning? Already it is hard to be quite sure. The emptiness of that silence, the void I felt then has receded from my mind and become dim. I know that gradually, over a number of days, and through the silence surrounding me, I began to hear sounds beyond the walls. It was the sound of a great ocean, the surge of a distant city. And close by I heard

80

my neighbour's dog bark shrilly. I suppose I finally moved because I needed to go to the bathroom, or thirst induced me to get up and fill the kettle while I considered the matter.

And now I have become accustomed to living my life. It happened almost too quickly, I think, and I miss the thrill of terror, the frightening silence with the sound of the ocean shaking through it. But I have developed my little habits. I no longer hear the silence, which is filled with the noise of a clock ticking, steam gushing as the kettle boils, birds cawing in winter trees, and my neighbour putting rubbish in the dustbin. Only the shrill sound of the telephone will remind me of the silence, bring it lapping back round me, as I wake from my dream. My children are strangers, very busy living their own lives. Occasionally they ring up to make sure I am not sick. Something in my voice disturbs them, but they do not know what it is. They become suspicious, and guilty, and think perhaps it is because they ring so rarely, and I know they vow to stop ringing up at all since my voice sounds odd, and makes them feel bad. Is something wrong, they ask, and hang up, and I cannot explain about the silence, how the harsh sound of the telephone startled me, and that I have become unused to speech.

Sometimes I still hear it, but not for long. I have my little habits, and the colouring book. I begin with the light coming through the gap in the curtains, and go on to the wardrobe, the dark oak chest and the long mirror. Once I get up and draw back the curtains I do not know what to expect, it is a constant source of surprise. What will it be this morning, misty, grey and brown seen through a light covering of cloud? I do not know. I could be startled by a large patch of blue sky, which in turn will colour what lies below, so that windows sparkle and a child's ball gleams bright blue on a dark muddy lawn. It is a comfort, living as I do now. And sometimes I still hear it, no more than a distant murmur heard now and then, through the silence, through the tinkle of tea-cups and the bark of my neighbour's dog, and I know it is still there, and recall the moment when I was deafened by it, when, thrilled and frightened by so much power, such emptiness, I seemed to hold it in my hands, to do with, what I could, even though it might, at that moment, have swept me off my feet. And perhaps I did. Who knows, perhaps I did.

7

The tide is out. How long have I been lying here? Dimly I see grey. It must be light. I lie at the bottom of a grey pool through which I see a dim light. I must try and move. The tide has thrown up a heavy rock, it is lying on me, I am pinned down. Mother, won't you come and lift me up? She is hiding from me, all of them, they want to frighten me, so I think I have been left behind. It hurts. Somehow I must lift myself upward, out of this salty pool, but I cannot move. I can taste the salt on my lips. I am hot, damp, small trickles of sea-water run down my neck and between my thighs. That dim light, it must be the sun. I can hear a titter of girlish laughter. They are hiding from me, so that if I call, nobody will come to help me. I must pull myself together, try and move, but I cannot find my limbs. Perhaps I am buried in sand, it has silted up overnight with that last tide, I will try and shift it. Please, come somebody

It is dark now, the tide is coming close. I hear the sound of ocean murmurs, coming close now, did somebody whisper, moan? No, I expect it is only the sound of dark waves running closer, I can feel a slight wind, cool on my face, it comes with the dark, with the sea pounding against rocks, I can hear it rushing in my head. Now I am tossed, thrown this way, and that, I am in terror of being thrown onto rough rocks, of being torn apart, but already the hollow in my head is filling with black liquid, gushing, moving dark shadows come, waver, my son, I cry out, but before I can utter two words he is swept away, and I am gasping for breath, trying to push the water out of my eyes. Will he come back to me, is he drowned? I see my daughter a small child filling her bucket in the dusk and I want to ask, why are you out so late, is it true there is nobody with you, but the black wave comes, now it is between us, hissing, now my head is full of it, swirling, gurgling, it will not come out, though I open my mouth nothing is heard

Now I am back in the silence. The dim light. Is it morning? I hear whispers, is it leaves stirring overhead, throwing their shadows on the wall? But the walls seem to have gone, or perhaps they are shining so much I do not see them now. I heard a cock crow, that was the first sound which broke the silence. But I do not hear it now. I have never heard it since. Perhaps a cock crows only once, at the beginning, after which the silence begins to close in once more. Yes, that would make sense. And if small birds twitter to the sound of sunrise that would hardly disturb the silence. Mother, can I get up? I cannot lift the bedclothes. How heavy they have become, suddenly. Please come soon, or the grass and the shadows will have dried up outside before I have had a chance to run through them. Already I am hot, too hot, and the walls have melted into light

It is dim. The light is becoming dim. I should go home now, the cold wind is blowing round my legs and my bucket is heavy, full of damp sand, I cannot lift it now, it hurts each time I try, I am gasping for breath and the air hurts as it goes in, sharp as a knife stabbing, while the sky is dying, light fading to the colour of metal, and in the silence, that queer little silence when the wind stops for a moment and I know there is nobody nearby I hear the whisper of the ocean, far distant but coming close, the sound is all around, mother, I call, why did you not wait for me, but I am not sure if I spoke and if so it was so faint the sound was lifted off by the wind and drowned. And now it picks me up bodily, I am tossed and turned in the black chaos, in my ears is silence, then sound, rushing into spaces, I have just time to think why did you leave me before the struggle becomes too much, I gasp for air, my head bobs up for a moment, out of dark water, but the night is black also, I am submerged, I must find my body which is helpless without me, without my head which is gasping for air up in the night where I thought I had just begun to make out a single star, a small point of light, just a pinprick in the black, but each necessary gasp brings a stab down below, which will not do, I belong to whatever is left down below in spite of the immense distances of blackness and moving space which have begun to open up in my head, and I can hear my lungs gurgling, I must help them, I think, breathing hard, in spite of the sharp stab on each occasion, or I will drown

Flat grey light. The tide has gone out, and all is very quiet. I am stretched out like flattened sand, damp and salty. I listen in the silence for the far murmur of the ocean, but hear nothing. I think perhaps I have been ill, but now it is peaceful. I am lying very still, hoping the sun will rise. Under my fingers I feel sand, dry now, and I remember to sift them through my hands to find by touch which of the grains could be crystal or diamond, ruby or another tiny emerald. So much

The walls have vanished. A blank white of sunlight through fog where the walls used to be, and my old sticks of furniture have also gone. Through the white room with no walls I hear voices, sighs and whispers, things moving, stirring, and now the clear sound of a cup ringing into its saucer

Shadows of leaves, a whole forest of leaves stirring around me, whispering, my head humming with hot insects while the sound of birds singing comes from above, from the sky which is full of leaf and branch. I dip my hand into the bucket, which is filled with clear cool water, and close my hand round the firm pebble lying on the bottom. It is hard in my palm, under the ring of

86

water my arm bends as though it had entered a queer world from which I am shut out

Now the light is fading. Is this air, or water? I would think it the evening tide, but if so the cool grey waves have crept round me with such stealth, so quietly, that I heard no sound. But I have known for some time that silence and the roar of the ocean were one and the same thing so I am neither alarmed nor surprised. Night falls above my head in the sky now that the ceiling is no longer visible. Everything has been washed away in the last tide, no more pain, now my body has been swept away I am light as a bird, no more trying to find bits of myself, the ache of effort with each breath, holding myself, pulling myself together like my poor old dislocated doll, how many years now, finding an arm, now a numb foot, pulling on aching muscles and stiff hot joints on first waking? Admit it, the hollow head, the mechanism for making the eyes open and shut could no longer be connected to the rest of it. The illusion was shattered. And now it has been washed away by the tide and I can float freely on the black waves, though I still hear the plaintive cry, mamma, each time it was tipped back, feeble but constant, unvarying in its timbre. And though the night is cool and the tide is creeping silently along the damp dark sand and I am not afraid, no, though the wind is rising over the dark horizon, the small voice in my head is crying mamma, why do you not come, why have you left me alone on the seashore with night coming in all round? But now I see a small light bobbing in the dark, it quivers, trembles, is it a spirit, no, the light of a

fishing boat putting out to sea on the far horizon, no,
perhaps a single star, the north star, rising in the sky,
but no, it is coming nearer, she has come for me, she
has not forgotten, she holds a torch in her hand, mamma,
she has come back to the seashore and I am safe, now
that she has come to fetch me, pick me up and carry me
home.

ABOUT THE AUTHOR

Eva Figes was born in Berlin, came to
England with her family just before the
outbreak of the Second World War, and
has lived here ever since. She graduated in
English language and literature at London
University and her first novel was
published in 1966. In 1967 she won the
Guardian Fiction Prize with her second
novel, and she has also published three
non-fiction books to date, a book on
tragedy, a memoir of her childhood and a
feminist book, *Patriarchal Attitudes*, first
published in 1970, which proved to be one
of the seminal books for the women's
movement. She is currently working on a
critical book on early women novelists.
Eva Figes is divorced and has two children,
a son and a daughter.